HOOP HUSTLE

BY JAKE MADDOX

Text by Brandon Terrell
Illustrated by Aburtov

STONE ARCH BOOKS
a capstone imprint

Jake Maddox Sports Stories are published by Stone Arch Books
A Capstone Imprint
1710 Roe Crest Drive
North Mankato, Minnesota 56003
www.capstonepub.com

Library of Congress Cataloging-in-Publication Data
Maddox, Jake, author. Hoop hustle / by Jake Maddox ; text by Josh Anderson ;
illustrated by Aburtov.

    pages cm. -- (Jake Maddox sports stories)

Summary: Brian Worth Jr. plans on trying out for his middle school's basketball
team, but the trouble is he has always relied on his height to give him an
advantage and that is no longer enough — but at the local senior center, where
he reluctantly volunteers, he discovers a friend in George, a former player, who
sets out to teach him some of the skills he is missing.

ISBN 978-1-4965-0494-4 (library binding) -- ISBN 978-1-4965-0498-2 (pbk.) --
ISBN 978-1-4965-2326-6 (ebook pdf) -- 978-1-4965-2468-3 (reflowable epub)

1. Basketball stories. 2. Confidence--Juvenile fiction. 3. Friendship--Juvenile
fiction. 4. Middle schools--Juvenile fiction. [1. Basketball--Fiction. 2. Self-
confidence--Fiction. 3. Friendship--Fiction. 4. Old age--Fiction. 5. Junior high
schools--Fiction. 6. Schools--Fiction.] I. Anderson, Josh, author. II. Aburto, Jesus,
illustrator. III. Title. IV. Series: Maddox, Jake. Impact books. Jake Maddox sports
story.

 PZ7.M25643Hn 2016
 813.6--dc23
 [Fic]

                        2014043710

Art Director: Bob Lentz
Graphic Designer: Veronica Scott
Production Specialist: Katy LaVigne

Printed in Canada
032015   008825FRF15

TABLE OF CONTENTS

CHAPTER 1

JUMP BALL

Brian Worth Jr. towered over everyone in the gym. Everyone except for Mike Barnes, that is. He stood across the center circle from Mike, staring him down. Mike was his biggest competition for the starting center position on varsity at Clinton Junior High.

Coach Van Schotten held the basketball. He blew his whistle and tossed the ball into the air for the tip-off. The two sixth graders leaped at the same time, but Mike took off fast and light. He reached the ball first and tipped it back to his team's point guard.

Brian shook his head in frustration and took off down the court. *I need to step up my game,* he thought as he ran back on defense. *I've been practicing for weeks, and I still haven't won a tip-off against Mike.*

Final cuts for the varsity squad were only a month away. Between now and the big scrimmage, which would happen right before cuts, Brian knew he had to do everything he could to impress the coach.

Only ten players would make varsity. The others would be stuck on JV. Making varsity was a huge deal for a sixth grader.

Mike stood with his back to Brian, setting up near the basket. Stevie, the team's point guard, dribbled the ball out by the three-point line. A few seconds later, Stevie threw a perfect pass to Mike, who dribbled the ball, pushing his body backward into Brian.

Mike turned on his right foot, used an elbow to keep Brian away, and put up a hook shot. Brian timed his jump perfectly, swatting the ball out of the air. Then he chased the ball down, dribbling as fast as he could until he was alone on the other side of the court, closing in on the hoop.

Brian switched hands for one more dribble, preparing for an easy layup. But when he looked up, he realized he'd gone past the basket. His only chance of scoring now was to try a reverse layup. He jumped and spun his body in the air, curling his arm under the backboard and releasing the ball. But it clanked off the bottom of the rim.

Coach blew his whistle, stopping the scrimmage. "Great block! Great hustle!" he called. "But Brian, if you look down while you dribble, you'll have no idea where you are on the court."

Brian felt his face get hot. In elementary school, his height and strong jump shot had made him the best player on the court. But at Clinton, all of Brian's teammates could shoot, and his height wasn't going to be enough to earn him a spot on varsity.

As Brian ran to get back on defense, he thought about his dad. Because his dad was professional basketball legend Brian "Slick" Worth Sr., Brian had always had a lot to prove on the court. Everyone was always comparing Brian to his dad.

But Brian didn't want to be known as "Slick Jr." He wanted to be his own person — and his own basketball player. *And it will all start with making varsity this season,* Brian thought.

CHAPTER 2

AFTER-PRACTICE PRACTICE

After practice, Brian headed toward home with three of his teammates: Mike, Stevie, and Patrick. He was quiet on the walk, dribbling a ball with his right hand. Every time he tried to look up, though, he dribbled the ball off his foot.

I can't have many more days like today if I want to keep my chance at varsity alive, he thought. *I'll have to put in more practice.*

"What do you guys say we play a quick game of two-on-two?" Stevie suggested as the group approached Seaview Park.

"I don't think I have time," Brian said. "I told my parents I'd be home by six."

Mike opened the gate to the park. "I'm in," he said.

Patrick followed Mike into the park. "Come on, Brian," he said. "It'll be quick."

Brian checked the time on his phone — quarter to six. *I guess I could get away with being five or ten minutes late,* he thought.

"All right, I'll play to seven," Brian said, following his friends onto the court known as the Moon for its uneven playing surface. "Patrick and me versus Stevie and Mike."

When Mike checked the ball to him, Brian felt confident in a way he hadn't all day.

Right away, Patrick screened Mike to clear a path for Brian to drive to the hoop. Brian gave a head fake to go left, dribbled to the right until he was close to the basket, and then stopped in front of Stevie for a short jumper. The rest of the first game went like that, and the final score wasn't even close. Brian and Patrick won easily, 7–2.

When Stevie insisted on playing another game, the result was the same. In fact, Brian owned the court, making crossovers, hitting jumpers, and grabbing rebounds all night. He just wished he could have the same swagger in the school gym.

It wasn't until the sun began to set that Brian realized he'd lost track of time. And he had a feeling he was going to be in trouble when he got home.

CHAPTER 3

BASKETBALL BALANCE

When Brian turned onto his block, he saw his normally relaxed father standing on the porch, talking loudly into his phone.

"He's here, Wanda . . . yes, he's here now. Come on home," Dad said, staring Brian down as he walked through the front gate.

Based on the tone of his dad's voice, Brian could tell he was in big trouble. His usual calm demeanor was part of what had made Brian Worth Sr. an all-star during his playing days. When he raised his voice, it wasn't a good sign.

"Sorry," Brian said quietly as he stepped onto the porch. "I was playing ball at the park and lost track of time."

"Don't you dare think you can use basketball as an excuse with me," Dad warned.

Brian stared at the ground. "I didn't realize how late it was," he mumbled.

"Why did we get you that cell phone then?" Dad asked. "Go upstairs. And don't come out of your room until we call for you."

* * *

An hour later, Brian's dad came into his room and handed him a plate with a turkey sandwich. "Do you realize how worried your mother and I were?" he asked. "What were you thinking?"

"I'm sorry. I had a bad practice and wanted to keep playing," Brian said, looking up at a poster of Michael Jordan on his wall. "Last year I was the best player on my team. And I still want to be the best."

"We want you to be the best, too," Dad agreed. "The best person. Basketball is not life. It's one part of life," Dad said. "But we know how important it is to you. That's why we're still going to let you go out for the team this year."

Brian breathed a sigh of relief. He hadn't even realized that not going out for the team was a possibility.

Dad must have been really upset, he thought.

"I'm really sorry, Dad," Brian said. "If there's anything I can do —"

"It's funny you should say that," Dad said. "Your mom and I came up with an idea. When I was playing college ball, my team used to visit the Senior Citizens' Center on Magnolia Avenue. It was a great way to give back to the community. And it was a good reminder that there is more to life than just basketball. So we decided that you're going to volunteer there two afternoons a week. You'll start tomorrow."

"What?" Brian asked. "What about basketball? I have practice tomorrow!"

"You'll still be able to go to practice. You'll just need to learn to budget your time. That means leaving practice promptly, volunteering at the Senior Center, and coming home right away to start on homework. It also means no extra practice in the park on weekdays," Dad said.

Brian couldn't believe it. *Dad, of all people, should understand putting basketball first,* he thought.

"How long do I have to do it?" Brian asked.

"At least through the fall," Dad said. "Now, do your homework."

Brian groaned.

"But hey, the weekend's coming up," Dad said. "We could play a little ball on Saturday during a homework break. I could show you some good ball fakes to use in the post."

"No thanks, Dad," Brian said.

It's what he always said when his dad offered hoops advice. *I need to figure the game out for myself,* he thought.

Brian wished his dad understood how hard it was to be the son of a basketball legend. He was already the spitting image of a young Slick Worth. If Slick was teaching him all his moves and skills, would Brian's game ever really be Brian's?

CHAPTER 4

AIRPLANES AND HOOPS

"I can tell from the look on your face that you'd rather be somewhere else," Ms. Schnabel, the volunteer director, said to Brian the next day as she led him down the hall of the Magnolia Senior Center.

"Sorry?" Brian said, surprised.

Sure, he was upset that he'd had to miss playing pick-up with his friends in the park, but he didn't think he'd done anything rude.

"I've seen a lot of volunteers," she said. "I can always tell the ones who want to be here from those who have to be here."

Ms. Schnabel stopped outside room 208. "This is George's room. I think you'll be a good match," she said. "George will be thrilled. His family lives far away, so he doesn't get many visitors. Any questions?"

Brian shook his head.

When Ms. Schnabel opened the door, Brian expected to see a room that looked as boring as the rest of the building. But as he walked in, Brian almost banged his head on a model airplane hanging from the ceiling.

"I forgot to tell you to watch your head," Ms. Schnabel said. "George makes all of these planes and likes to display them around the room."

George looked up from a table covered with model parts. He didn't look anything like what Brian had expected. He didn't look weak or sick at all.

"You like planes?" George asked.

"Uh . . . sure," Brian said. "I guess."

George held up the model he was working on. "You know what this one is?" he asked as Ms. Schnabel left the room.

Brian shrugged. "No clue."

"It's an F-105 Thunderchief," George said. "Weighed fifty-thousand pounds but could fly at the speed of sound. And that one hanging by the door was called the Aardvark for its long nose. The F-111."

Brian stood in the doorway with his hands in his pockets. "Cool," he said.

"You wanna sit?" George asked.

"I'm okay," Brian said.

"You look like you're getting ready to leave," George said.

"Well, I have to be home by five-thirty," Brian replied.

"It's barely half past four," George said. "Where do you live, China? Come chat for a minute."

Brian reluctantly walked over to George and sat down on a chair beside him.

"So, what's your thing?" George asked.

"Huh?" Brian said.

"What's your thing?" George said again. "What is it that you think about when you wake up in the morning or when you're supposed to be listening in math class?"

"Basketball," Brian said. "It's my favorite thing in the world."

George smiled and leaned back in his chair. "That must be why they paired us up then," he said. "I have played a little ball in my time."

"Cool," Brian said. He paused for a minute, trying to think of something else to say. When he couldn't think of anything, he said, "Well, I'd better get going. Lots of homework tonight. I'll be back on Friday, though."

"I'll be here," George said.

Brian stood up, waved goodbye, and quickly left the room, heading out of the Senior Center as fast as he could.

CHAPTER 5

CENTER MENTOR

Brian had been playing terribly all week. On defense, he'd been missing switches, adjustments to make sure no player on the other team is left open, and he had been given multiple three-second violations for standing too long in the paint, the area beneath the basket.

On offense, Brian had been missing layups and short jumpers that he would typically hit — if his shots weren't blocked first.

After Friday's less-than-stellar practice, Brian rushed out the door. He had to get to the Senior Center in time to put in two volunteer hours.

If he didn't, he would have to go back over the weekend. And Brian couldn't afford to lose any more practice time.

* * *

Wishing he were practicing instead, Brian reluctantly knocked on George's door. George opened it, and Brian looked up, surprised at how tall the older man was.

"Your dad played for Phoenix," George said without greeting him. "I did some research. I thought your name sounded familiar."

"And Milwaukee," Brian said, walking into the room.

"I bet you're good!" George said. "You're tall, too. Do you play center?"

Brian put down his backpack. After his terrible practice, he wasn't in the mood to talk basketball. He nodded in response. "Yup. That's my position."

"That was my position, too. You got a hook shot?" George asked. "It was my claim to fame."

"Nah," said Brian, shaking his head.

"How come your dad never taught you a hook?" George asked. "You're not born with that skill, you know!"

George paused, then stood up and headed for the door. "You've got to have a hook shot," he said. "Why don't you come with me to the rec room. Humor an old man."

After hesitating a minute, Brian followed George down the hallway. *I did just have a terrible practice,* he thought. *It couldn't hurt to get in some more court time.*

The rec room looked straight out of the 1970s. There was a shuffleboard court, some ancient-looking exercise bikes, and a rusty basketball hoop with a masking tape outline for a backboard bolted to the wall.

George picked up a ball from a nearby bin and bounced it against the wood floor. "Love that sound," he said, smiling.

Suddenly the older man tossed a sharp chest pass to Brian. The ball came at him much faster than Brian had expected.

"You want me to shoot?" Brian asked.

"Go ahead and post me up," George said.

"Really?" Brian asked.

George nodded, so Brian turned his back to the older man and started dribbling. When he came into contact with George, Brian quickly backed off. "Sorry," he said.

"I'm 73, not 103," George said. "Now post me up for real, and try a hook shot."

Brian pivoted on his right foot and flung the ball up toward the basket. It grazed the rim, but the shot missed.

"Take your time," George said. "Use your arm to create space between us."

Brian tried again. This time, his shot rattled around the rim and went in.

"Better," George said. "Watch me."

Before Brian knew what was happening, George posted up, pivoting and extending his forearm into Brian's chest with enough power to push him back a few steps.

George took a shot with his right hand, barely leaving the ground. The ball fell cleanly through the hoop.

"The key," George said, "is taking the time to get a good look. People think a hook shot means you're not looking at the basket, but you just start the shot that way. Using your forearm to create space will give you time for a good look." He passed the ball to Brian. "Now let's see you try."

CHAPTER 6

NOTHING BUT NET

After practicing for a good hour, Brian went back to George's room to grab his backpack before heading home. Before he could leave, though, George bent down to grab a metal box from under his bed. "Hold on a sec. Let me show you something," he said, opening the box and pulling out an old issue of *Sports Illustrated*.

He opened the magazine to a black-and-white photo of a basketball game and turned it around for Brian to see.

"That's me right there," he said. "It's been fifty years, and Canarsie State hasn't been back to the Final Four."

"Cool photo," Brian said.

"If not for the war, I might've gone pro," George said. "Would you like to take this home to read? It might be interesting to hear how the game was played in my day."

"Uh . . . no thanks," Brian said.

"C'mon. You might learn something," George said.

"That's okay," Brian said firmly. The truth was, he didn't want to read some boring old article about the Final Four from forever ago. It felt like George was giving him homework, and he already had enough of that.

George shrugged. "Suit yourself," he said.

* * *

The next day at practice, Brian decided to try out the hook shot he and George had practiced. He caught a pass in the post from Stevie and felt Mike, who was defending him as usual, at his back. Brian dribbled twice and instead of trying a head fake, he pivoted and put up the hook shot.

Mike tried to block it, but Brian's forearm had created the space he needed to get the shot off.

His first try missed, but as the scrimmage went on, Brian was hitting more and more hook shots.

"Very nice, Brian!" Coach Van Schotten called from the sidelines. "Now let's try mixing the hook in with some of your other moves."

The rest of practice felt like a dream to Brian. Not only were his hook shots going in, but everything he put up seemed to fall through the net. The confidence he was gaining from hitting his shots seemed to carry over to his defense, too. Brian had three nice blocks in the last few minutes of practice.

As he walked off the court, Brian realized that making varsity suddenly seemed like it was within reach.

CHAPTER 7

FAST BREAK

When Brian showed up at the Senior Center the following Tuesday, he and George headed straight to the gym. Even though he had mastered the hook shot, Brian knew he still needed to work on some skills.

I just wish I could get better faster, he thought as they walked down the hall.

"Want to learn how to throw a perfect outlet pass?" George asked, pushing the gym door open.

"What's an outlet pass?" Brian asked, picking up a stray basketball. He passed it to George.

"I'm glad you asked," George said. "It's a pass you can use to move the ball quickly down the court, like when you're setting your teammate up for a fast break to the hoop."

He dribbled over to the free throw line and shot the basketball, missing on purpose.

"Like this," he said as he caught the rebound and pivoted around. "Now you run along the sideline, and I'll send this down the court in front of you — kind of like a long football pass."

Brian took off down the sideline, and George threw the ball far ahead of him. For a moment, Brian thought he wouldn't catch up to it.

But when he was several feet away from the basket, Brian caught the pass, took two dribbles toward the basket, and went in strong for a layup. The ball bounced off the backboard and fell cleanly through the net.

* * *

After they had practiced for a good hour, Brian and George walked back to George's room. Brian was quiet, embarrassed to say what was on his mind. *It'd be great to practice some more before the scrimmage,* he thought. *And playing with George is so much less pressure than playing with Dad.* Finally he spoke up. "Final cuts are coming up. Do you think I could come a couple extra times next week so we can practice some more?"

"Hmm . . . next week might be a little tough for me. But we'll see. This week, though, I'm free as a bird," George said.

CHAPTER 8

UPDATE

As the week went by, Brian was getting more and more nervous about proving to Coach that he deserved to be on varsity. Time was passing quickly, and the big scrimmage was only two weeks away, so Brian went to visit and practice with George several times.

On Thursday, they practiced ball fakes. On Friday, they practiced free throws. And on Sunday, they practiced jump shots and ball handling.

But when Brian showed up on Tuesday after practice, George was nowhere to be found. After knocking on George's door for a couple minutes, Brian walked down to Ms. Schnabel's office and peeked his head inside her door. "Excuse me," he said.

"Oh, Brian!" Ms. Schnabel said. "Nice to see you. Did you come to get an update on George?"

"Update?" Brian asked.

"Oh, dear," Ms. Schnabel said. "No one told you?"

Brian got a nervous feeling in his stomach.

"George had surgery yesterday," she said. "We thought he'd be back from the hospital by now, but he had some trouble breathing, so they want to keep him a bit longer."

"Will he be okay?" Brian asked, stunned.

George had surgery? Why didn't he say something? he wondered.

"We hope so," she said.

"Can I go see him?" Brian asked.

"I don't think that's such a good idea, honey," Ms. Schnabel said. "I've got your phone number. Once I get an update from his family, I promise I'll tell you everything I know."

Brian walked out of Ms. Schnabel's office quickly, his eyes filled with tears. He'd just met George — now he was afraid he might never see him again.

CHAPTER 9

SLICK MOVES

When he got home, Brian went right to his room. He had no appetite after hearing the news about George.

"Is everything okay, kiddo?" Dad asked, poking his head through the doorway. "Do you want to talk about it?"

Brian shook his head. Talking was the last thing he wanted to do. *There's only one thing that might cheer me up . . . basketball. But now I don't have George to play with,* he thought.

But then another thought crossed his mind.

Before his dad started down the stairs, Brian called, "Hey, Dad! Want to go shoot some hoops?"

Dad popped his head back through the doorway and smiled. "Sure. Meet you out there in five?"

* * *

Out in the driveway, Brian dribbled once, stopped quickly, and threw up a quick jumper. He watched it rattle in. 1–0.

On the next possession, Brian backed into his dad in the post. He was able to score with a hook shot, and he could see his dad was impressed. Now Brian was up by two.

"Hey, I've never seen that shot from you before," Dad said, passing the ball to Brian.

Brian didn't reply. Instead, he faked a shot before trying to drive around his dad. Unfortunately, he dribbled the ball off of his foot, and it rolled out of bounds.

Brian's dad took possession and hit three jump shots in a row to take the lead before driving around Brian and leaping up to try a slam-dunk. Luckily for Brian, his dad missed the dunk, and Brian chased down the rebound. He was down 2–3.

Brian drove straight to the rim and lofted a layup over his dad, tying the game at three.

This is actually pretty fun, Brian thought. *Maybe I should play ball with Dad more often.*

On the next possession, Brian tried the shot again. But this time, his dad was ready for it.

Slick timed it perfectly, jumping up and swatting the ball out of the air. Then he chased down the ball and put up a graceful jumper, bringing the score to 3–4.

"Tonight's not gonna be the night, son," Brian Sr. said.

When Brian checked the ball, he had a feeling his dad was going to try to dunk again to win the game. But Brian was ready.

Slick started to move to the hoop, and instead of trying to poke his hand in for a steal, Brian let his dad pass him. Then he turned and ran as fast as he could toward the rim.

As his dad elevated for the easy slam, Brian leaped into the air too, reaching his arm out as far as he could.

But his hand slammed against the backboard a second too late, and Dad's dunk swished through the net.

"Look at those hops," Dad said. "You're gonna do some damage against kids your own age." He smiled. "Speaking of which, you've got that big scrimmage coming up on Saturday, right?"

Brian nodded and leaned over to catch his breath. He had lost the game, but it was the first time he'd even come close to beating his dad.

Maybe I'm more ready for the scrimmage than I gave myself credit for, Brian thought.

"Catch your breath," Dad said. "I know a great box-out drill we can do."

CHAPTER 10

COURT COMPETITION

The week passed slowly. Brian kept waiting for Ms. Schnabel to call with an update on George, but the call never came. Practice was going well, and Coach was noticing Brian's improvement, but Brian was still nervous for the big scrimmage.

When Brian walked into the gym on Saturday morning, there were lots of people in the stands — mostly friends and families of the players. Brian's parents sat a few rows up. As Brian looked up at them and waved, he felt a little knot in his stomach.

Whenever Brian's dad was there to watch, it made Brian want to play a little bit better.

The team had been split into two groups, and every player was well aware that this open scrimmage was their final chance to show Coach that they belonged on varsity.

After all the starting players gathered around the center jump circle, the referee tossed the jump ball. Brian timed his jump perfectly. But when he flicked his wrist to tip the ball, it wasn't there. Mike had beaten him to it — again.

Much of the first half played out like the jump ball. Brian played okay, but Mike played great. Brian could feel his confidence dipping again. He knew he needed to get it back or else he could kiss varsity goodbye.

Right before halftime, Brian had a chance to tie the game. He backed Mike down in the post, setting up for a move to the hoop. But as Brian took one last dribble, the ball hit his foot and rolled out toward the three-point line.

Brian dove on the floor, trying to save the possession, but Mike got there first. All he could do was watch as Mike dribbled the length of the court, graceful as a gazelle, and drove toward the hoop for an easy layup.

* * *

At halftime, Brian sat on the bench with his head in his hands, disappointed that Mike had outplayed him yet again.

If I can't be my best today, Brian thought, *maybe I don't deserve varsity.*

Just then, a voice came from behind Brian. "Cheer up, kid. There are worse places you could be — like say, the hospital."

Brian turned and couldn't believe his eyes. It was George! He was in a wheelchair, but he was there.

George wheeled closer to the bench. "Sorry I'm a little late," he said. "How'd the first half go?"

"Not so great," Brian admitted. "I can't believe you're here. How are you feeling?"

"Don't worry about me. Worry about varsity," George said. "You have all the tools you need. If Brian from the first half wasn't the Brian you want everyone to see, then show 'em someone twice as good in the second half."

The whistle blew calling the players back to the court.

"Thanks for coming, George," Brian said.

"I'll stick around for the second half, but I have to head out right after the game ends," George said. "Come see me Monday, will ya? Let me know how it all turns out."

"Definitely," Brian said. He turned back to the court and headed out for the start of the second half.

* * *

Maybe Brian was energized knowing that George was there, or maybe it was a stroke of good luck. Whatever it was, Brian turned things around in the second half. His jumps were a little higher, his passes a little crisper, and his shots found the basket again and again.

During the first half, Brian had felt more like the player he'd been a month ago. But after halftime, the new-and-improved Brian was back.

Brian was boxing out on defense and going after the rebounds on offense. He was quick on defense, and even made a few steals off of sloppy passes. On one play, Brian knocked a soft pass out of the air right in front of Mike, then grabbed hold of it and sent an arcing outlet pass down the court to Stevie. Brian's entire team played well, and although they lost, the final score was close — 34–31.

Even though Brian would have no idea whether he'd earned a spot on varsity until Monday, when Coach would post the roster at school, he walked off the court feeling prouder than he ever had before.

CHAPTER 11

DECISION TIME

On Monday, the first day back at school after Saturday's big scrimmage, Brian checked the bulletin board outside Coach's office after every class.

It wasn't until the end of the school day that Brian finally got his answer. As he approached the bulletin board, Brian took a deep breath. He was ready for anything. He'd given varsity his best shot, and now it was out of his hands. He read the note: "CONGRATULATIONS TO THIS YEAR'S CLINTON VARSITY BASKETBALL TEAM."

Brian scanned the list, and his heart sank when he saw Mike's name at the top. *Is it possible that Coach put both of us on varsity?* he wondered. He kept reading the names slowly, one by one, until he finally got the answer.

Brian's heart started pounding. *I have to go see George right away,* he thought.

* * *

Brian couldn't wait to share the news as he hurried down the hall of the Senior Center and knocked on George's door.

"Come in!" George called.

Brian pushed open the door and stood there, shell-shocked. Basketball-shaped balloons hung from the ceiling, and a big congratulations sign was on the wall. George was still in his wheelchair, but he'd somehow managed to decorate his whole room.

w'd you know?" Brian asked.

could barely sleep thinking about it,"
ge said. "So I called your coach to ask."

Brian smiled. "How are you feeling?"

"Better now," George said, sliding over a round orange cake. "Eat some of this. The doctors won't let me have sugar."

Brian ate his cake, and he and George talked about basketball. Suddenly, Brian remembered something. "Remember when you said I could borrow that magazine?" he asked. "Can I?"

"You're just being nice to an old man," George said, smiling.

"No, I really want to," Brian said.

"Well, okay," George said. "So long as you promise we'll get back on the court as soon as I recover."

"You got it," Brian said.

"You said that other center made the team too, right?" George asked.

Brian nodded. "Yep — Mike. So one of us will see a lot of bench time."

"How long before the first game of the season?" George asked.

"Three weeks," Brian answered.

"Then we don't have much time to convince Coach that you should be the one starting at center. Brian Worth Jr. certainly isn't a benchwarmer."

Brian smiled. "You have any more moves you can teach me?"

"Plenty," George said.

AUTHOR BIO

Josh Anderson is the author of several sports-themed books for kids. He lives and works in the Los Angeles area with his wife, Corey, and their two big guys, Leo and Dane.

ILLUSTRATOR BIO

Aburtov has worked as a colorist for Marvel, DC, IDW, and Dark Horse and as an illustrator for Stone Arch Books. He lives in Monterrey, Mexico, with his lovely wife, Alba, and his crazy children, Ilka, Mila, and Aleph.

GLOSSARY

adjustments (uh-JUHST-ments) — small changes made to make something work better

competition (kom-puh-TISH-uhn) — a contest, or a situation in which two or more people are trying to get the same thing

confidence (KON-fi-duhnss) — a feeling or belief that you will do something well

forearm (FOR-arm) — the part of your arm from your wrist to your elbow

hustle (HUHSS-uhl) — to work quickly and energetically

impress (im-PRESS) — to make people think highly of you

improvement (im-PROOV-ment) — the state of being better than before

professional (pruh-FESH-uh-nuhl) — in sports, making money for doing something others do for fun

reverse (ri-VURS) — opposite in position, order, or direction

scrimmage (SKRIM-ij) — an informal game, often done for practice

swagger (SWAG-ur) — to walk or act in a bold way

violations (VYE-uh-LAY-shuhns) — acts of breaking rules

volunteer (vol-uhn-TEER) — to offer to do a job, usually without pay

DISCUSSION QUESTIONS

1. Do you think Brian made the right choice when he decided to get in some extra practice with his friends at Seaview Park? Discuss why or why not.

2. Why do you think George is so interested in helping Brian succeed? Talk about the possibilities.

3. Was it fair of Brian's dad to make him volunteer at the senior center for disobeying? Talk about whether or not you think it was a fair punishment.

WRITING PROMPTS

1. Brian admires his dad for his talent on the court, but even so, he doesn't want to be compared to him. Why do you think that is? Write a paragraph about the possible reasons.

2. Imagine that Brian doesn't make the varsity team. What happens next? Write a different ending to this story.

3. George wants to share a magazine article with Brian about his best basketball days. Do some research about how the game of basketball has changed over the past fifty years, and write a magazine article about George's college team.

BASKETBALL DICTIONARY

- **boxing out** — a technique used to help players rebound; the player who is boxing out, usually the player on defense, maintains bodily contact with the offensive player he is guarding and stands between the competitor and the basket.

- **fast break** — a quick offensive drive to the basket, attempting to beat the defense down the court

- **free throw** — also known as a foul shot, free throws are awarded after a player is fouled by someone on the opposing team. The free throw is an unopposed attempt to score points from the area known as the foul line. Each free throw is worth one point.

- **hook shot** — a shot made by swinging your arm up and over your head

- **jump ball** — a method of putting a basketball into play; the referee throws the basketball into the air between two opposing players, who jump up and attempt to direct it to a teammate.

- **jump shot** — a shot made while jumping and releasing the ball at the peak of your jump

- **layup** — a two-point shot made from very close to the basket, usually by bouncing the ball off the backboard

- **outlet pass** — a throw of the ball from the defensive rebounder to a teammate for a fast break

- **paint** — the area on a basketball court underneath the basket and bounded by the end line, the foul line, and other lines. The inside of the area is painted. This area is where much of the action takes place.

- **post up** — to take up a position in the post, the area underneath and close to the basket, against a defender with your back facing the basket

- **rebound** — to catch the basketball after a shot has been missed

- **screen** — a move by an offensive player to block a defensive player in order to free up a teammate to pass, shoot, get open, or drive to the basket

- **switch** — adjustments made by the team on defense, usually after the offense performs a screen

- **three-pointer** — a successful shot from outside the designated arc of the three-point line on a basketball court, as opposed to the typical two-point shot for baskets made inside the arc

- **three-second rule** — a defensive violation in which a player spends more than three seconds in the free-throw lane, or the paint, while not actively guarding a player

4 NEW BOOKS!
• HOOP HUSTLE
• CAUGHT STEALING
• SOCCER SHAKE-UP
• TOUCHDOWN TRIUMPH
FIND MORE AT CAPSTONEPUB.COM

READ THEM ALL !

DATE DUE